Phonics Fun
Reading Program [Book 11: r, -op]

Clifford
Is Tops

by Grace Maccarone

Illustrated by Carolyn Bracken
and Ken Edwards

Based on the books by Norman Bridwell

SCHOLASTIC INC.
New York   Toronto   London   Auckland   Sydney
Mexico City   New Delhi   Hong Kong   Buenos Aires

My pop had a red car.
The red car did not go.
"Oh, no!" said Pop.

I said, "Stop, Clifford."

I said, "Drop, Clifford.
Help my pop."

I said, "Hop on, Pop."
My pop was up, up, up!

Clifford ran and ran.

He ran with Pop on top.

Pop got to the shop where Mom was.

Clifford ran home to me
with Mom and Pop.

I said, "Drop, Clifford.
Come down, Mom.
Come down, Pop."

Clifford is tops!